SO-APY-554

Growing Up in
China

Other titles in the *Growing Up Around the World* series include:

Growing Up in
China

John Allen

San Diego, CA

For more information, contact:
ReferencePoint Press, Inc.
PO Box 27779
San Diego, CA 92198
www.ReferencePointPress.com

LIBRARY OF CONGRESS CATALOGING-IN-PUBLICATION DATA

Name: Allen, John, 1957– author.
Title: Growing Up in China/by John Allen.
Description: San Diego, CA: ReferencePoint Press, Inc., 2018. | Series:
  Growing Up Around the World | Includes bibliographical references and
  index.
Identifiers: LCCN 2017026701 (print) | LCCN 2017027266 (ebook) | ISBN
  9781682822104 (eBook) | ISBN 9781682822098 (hardback)
Subjects: LCSH: Youth--China—Social life and customs—21st century. |
  Youth—China—Social conditions—21st century. | China—Social
  conditions—21st century. | China—Economic conditions—21st century. |
  China—Religion—21st century.
Classification: LCC HQ799.C55 (ebook) | LCC HQ799.C55 A734 2018 (print) | DDC
  305.2350951--dc23
LC record available at https://lccn.loc.gov/2017026701

CONTENTS

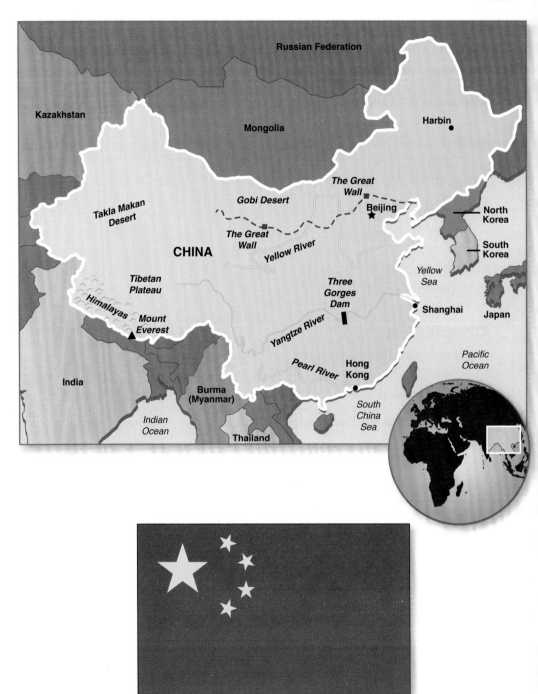

Official Name
People's Republic of China

Size
3,705,407 square miles (9,596,960 sq. km)

Total Population
1,373,541,278

Youth Population
0–14 years: 17.1%
15–24 years: 13.27%

Religion
Buddhist: 18.2%; Christian: 5.1%;
Muslim: 1.8%; folk religion: 21.9%;
unaffiliated: 52.2%

Capital
Beijing

Type of Government
Communist state

Languages
Standard Chinese or Mandarin
(official; Putonghua, based on
Beijing dialect); Yue (Cantonese);
Wu (Shanghainese); Minbei
(Fuzhou); Minnan (Hokkien Taiwanese);
Xiang, Gan, Hakka dialects

Currency
Renminbi (Chinese) yuan

Industries
Mining and ore processing; iron, steel,
aluminum, and other metals; coal; machine
building; armaments; textiles and apparel;
petroleum; cement; chemicals; fertilizers;
consumer products (including footwear)

Literacy
96.4% (age 15+ able to read and write)

Internet Users
731 million, or 53.2% of population

CHAPTER ONE

A Rising Nation

In December 2016 the death of American actor Alan Thicke brought a flood of sympathetic posts on Chinese social media. Many young Chinese had grown up in the 1990s watching Thicke play a kindly father in the suburbs on the American sitcom *Growing Pains*. As one of the first American shows to reach China, it struck young viewers with the contrast between the culture and lifestyle it displayed and the traditional fare they saw on Chinese state television. The show represented the first trickle in a flood of Western pop culture that has washed over China in the ensuing years. The very title—*Growing Pains*—fit the situation in which young Chinese found themselves. They were coming of age in a nation torn between the brutality of its recent Communist past and an uncertain future featuring new economic opportunities and engagement with the West.

For their part, China's leaders today are suspicious of the West's allure. Polls in the past decade indicate that many Chinese college students prefer certain ideas of liberal democracy to the one-party system of the Chinese state. In 2011, then-president Hu Jintao likened Western pop culture to a plot by hostile forces. "Ideological and cultural fields are the focal areas of [the West's] long-term infiltration," he said. "The international culture of the West is strong while we are weak."[1] Judging by the outpouring of grief prompted by Thicke's death, the influence of Western culture in China is not likely to subside anytime soon. And this will certainly affect the outlook for millions of Chinese youth.

A Quarter of the World's People

Children in China grow up learning about the vastness of their nation, both in size and population. The People's Republic of China is the world's third-largest country in territory and the largest overall in number of people. More than one of every six people in the world lives in China. Located in eastern Asia on the western shores of the Pacific Ocean, China is larger than the United States and Europe combined, with an area of 9.6 million square kilometers (3.7 million square miles).

To those outside China, the nation summons images of the past, from the Great Wall to the Forbidden City complex of palaces to the beautiful artifacts of porcelain and silk produced over the centuries. Yet in recent decades China has rapidly caught up with the modern world. Large cities like Beijing and Shanghai are filled with glittering skyscrapers and spires out of a science fiction film. Flashing LED signs, most in Chinese characters but a fair

People shop on Nanjing Road in Shanghai, one of the busiest retail shopping areas in the world. In recent decades, China has caught up with the modern world with its large city skylines and constant streams of traffic.

number in English, light up the evening sky and flow down the sides of buildings. A constant stream of traffic, including automobiles, trucks, buses, bicycles, and pedestrians, attests to a busy populace. Financial houses trade shares in companies worth billions of yuan, the Chinese currency. A growing class of financiers and entrepreneurs amass great wealth via the nation's booming economy. Factories produce all kinds of consumer goods—such as clothes, shoes, toys, kitchenware, and mobile phones—both for domestic use and export. Urban dwellers race to obtain the best jobs, the best apartments, the best clothes and schools for their children, the best vacations, and the latest computerized

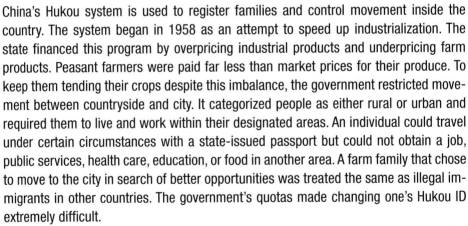

The Hukou System

China's Hukou system is used to register families and control movement inside the country. The system began in 1958 as an attempt to speed up industrialization. The state financed this program by overpricing industrial products and underpricing farm products. Peasant farmers were paid far less than market prices for their produce. To keep them tending their crops despite this imbalance, the government restricted movement between countryside and city. It categorized people as either rural or urban and required them to live and work within their designated areas. An individual could travel under certain circumstances with a state-issued passport but could not obtain a job, public services, health care, education, or food in another area. A farm family that chose to move to the city in search of better opportunities was treated the same as illegal immigrants in other countries. The government's quotas made changing one's Hukou ID extremely difficult.

In 2001, when China joined the World Trade Organization, new markets for textiles and clothing led to a huge demand for labor in urban Chinese factories. The state issued new Hukou permits to allow the flow of rural workers to cities. Patrols and passport inspections were eased somewhat. Yet today Hukou regulations still place a special burden on migrant youths in cities like Beijing. "The Hukou . . . makes it hard for them to assimilate," says Sharron Lovell, a reporter in China. "They're denied the rights and status of city dwellers and struggle to access social services."

Sharron Lovell, "Urban Migration for Young Chinese on the Rise," *PBS NewsHour*, July 12, 2012. www.pbs.org.

gadgets for their homes. Prosperous young people in the cities have the world at their fingertips via their smartphones (or at least as much of the world as their government allows them to see). They soak in the latest music, films, fashions, fads, and celebrity news like kids the world over.

Despite this wave of growth and prosperity, much of China remains tied to old ideas and traditions. Confucianism, a philosophy that dates back to before the Christian era, still holds sway with its emphasis on patience, discipline, self-control, and respect for elders. Away from the city, life is ruled by the change of seasons, as it has been for centuries. In rural villages farmers tend their fields just as their parents and grandparents did. Children are taught the value of hard work and the wisdom of being frugal. Most of these villages have yet to benefit from the recent economic boom, pointing up the growing inequality among people and regions in China. This promises to be a major issue for today's young Chinese, regardless of where they live in this vast nation.

A Varied Geography and Climate

With its sprawling landmass, China's geography is quite diverse. It is bordered by North and South Korea to the east; Mongolia to the north; Russia to the northeast; Kazakhstan, Kyrgyzstan, and Tajikistan to the northwest; Afghanistan, Pakistan, and India to the west and southwest; and Vietnam, Laos, and Myanmar to the south. China's coastline extends for 9,010 miles (about 14,500 km). Along its eastern shore lies the Pacific Ocean, and farther south is the South China Sea. Western China contains mostly mountains, high plateaus, and deserts. Areas in central and eastern China slope down into broad plains and river deltas. Major rivers include the Yangtze—at 3,964 miles (6,380 km) the longest river in Asia and the third longest in the world—the Yellow, and the Pearl. The Himalayas, the world's tallest mountain range, extend along the southwestern border. The Gobi Desert, which has an area of about 500,000 square miles (1.3 million sq. km), is a cold wasteland that runs west to east along the northern border with Mongolia.

China has a climate that also varies greatly depending on the region. In general much of the nation experiences a warm climate with distinct seasons. Northeastern China has dry, hot summers and extremely cold winters. Moist winds blowing from the sea make most other regions of China stiflingly hot and rainy in summer. The plains of central China, particularly the agricultural areas along the Yangtze, are known for humid summers and large amounts of rainfall. Southeastern China also gets plenty of rainfall and has semitropical summers and winters that are pleasantly cool. Flooding is frequent in central, southern, and western China. The Tibetan plateau to the west, surrounded by mountain ranges, has frost in its southern region for six months of the year and bitterly cold temperatures year round in the higher northern areas. The capital city of Beijing is located in the plain of northern China, where spring and autumn are brief but colorful.

China has one of the most diverse collections of wildlife on Earth. It contains 6,266 species of vertebrates—10 percent of the world's total. More than one hundred species of wild animals are unique to China. The most famous of these, and beloved by Chinese schoolchildren, is the giant panda. The panda is native to the southwestern region, along with bamboo, its main food source. Three species of golden monkeys live in the forests and mountains of Yunnan, Sichuan, and Guizhou Provinces. Like the giant panda, golden monkeys are endangered due to the destruction of their living areas. Chinese alligators, which make their home in the freshwater streams and tributaries of the lower Yangtze, also are faced with extinction in the wild. Among the more than thirty thousand plant species found in China are the golden larch, which is native to the Yangtze valley; the dove tree, also called the ghost tree, with flowers whose petals look like the wings of a dove; and the gutta-percha tree, a small native variety with leaves useful in the rubber industry and bark that has medicinal properties. China's forests hold many wild species of plants, but the spread of cities, factories, and grazing areas for livestock threatens their natural cycle of regeneration and development.

China also ranks third in the world in mineral reserves, including coal, aluminum, copper, iron, lead, zinc, and mercury. A large percentage of the world's rare earth minerals are mined in China. These are extremely rare substances used for consumer electronics, wind turbines, and other high-tech purposes.

China has one of the most diverse collections of wildlife on Earth. More than one hundred species are unique to China. Most famous of these is the giant panda.

Young People on the Move

One of China's greatest resources is its younger generation. Young people under age thirty make up about 30 percent of this rising nation's enormous population, with a little more than 18 percent at age fourteen or younger in 2015. This relatively small percentage of youths today is the result of China's strict family planning policy, which was introduced in 1979. In order to curb the nation's rapid population growth, the Communist rulers announced harsh penalties for couples who had more than one child. In 2015 this policy began to be phased out in favor of a two-child limit. Nonetheless, experts warn that the effects will be felt for decades to come. Ye Tingfang, a professor at the Chinese Academy of Social Sciences, insists it is unnatural for

13

a child to lack siblings or cousins as playmates. He and certain colleagues had long recommended that the government abolish the one-child policy. "It is not healthy for children to play only with their parents and be spoiled by them," he said several years ago. "It is not right to limit the number [of children] to two, either."[2] According to demographic researchers, there are signs that China's fertility rates would have fallen anyway, regardless of the one-child policy, judging by the drop in birthrates in other countries with strong, stable economies. In any case, China today has a labor shortage of young workers and a population that is aging overall.

> "It is not healthy for children to play only with their parents and be spoiled by them."[2]
>
> —Ye Tingfang, a professor at the Chinese Academy of Social Sciences, on China's one-child policy

Young people in China lead widely varied lives depending on where they live. A Chinese youth might work at a busy neighborhood restaurant located in an alley in Guangzhou, a large manufacturing city in southeastern China. He or she might work long hours assembling cell phones or computer game consoles at a factory on the outskirts of Shanghai. A recent college graduate in Beijing might create his or her own export business, reaching customers around the world. Young people in China's coastal south might help tend to family crops, work in chemical factories, or seek jobs teaching in village schools.

Overall, China's younger generation is moving from farms to cities. By 2020 an estimated 100 million people will have relocated to urban areas in only five years. By 2026 that number is expected to rise to 250 million. Newly arrived young workers tend to settle on the outskirts of large cities, where conditions are slightly less crowded and living expenses are cheaper. "It's a new world for us in the city," says Tian Wei, a young Chinese man who moved from wheat farming country to a big-city job as a factory watchman. "All my life I've worked with my hands in the fields; do I have the educational level to keep up with the city people?"[3] To accommodate the flood of new workers, the Chinese government races to construct the necessary highways, bridges, mass transportation outlets, and utilities for the settlements. Changes that once would have taken place over decades are planned for a matter of months or a few years.

A woman walks down a Beijing street with her son. In 2015, China began phasing out its longtime one-child-per-couple policy in favor of a two-child limit as officials are now striving to expand the youth population.

Shrinking Population and Labor Shortages

For a young person in China—particularly someone raised in a slower-paced rural area—daily life in a large city can seem disorienting and unstable, proceeding at breakneck speed. A section manager in his midtwenties at an automobile factory in Chongqing, one of the world's fastest-growing cities, enjoys his work but also feels the stress. "[I] am under great pressure now, because there is fierce competition in the market," he says. "We are producing the best car and I have to contribute more."[4] He hopes he might even be able to afford one of those cars himself at some point.

With China's working-age population actually shrinking due to earlier one-child family policies, labor shortages in manufacturing towns are increasingly common. The result has been higher pay for factory jobs—another attraction for rural youths. Young people from the countryside who obtain factory work in large cities find themselves entering a new world. A Chinese girl at one factory describes the feeling of entering a secret society:

When you met a girl from another factory, you quickly took her measure. *What year are you?* you asked each other, as if speaking not of human beings but of the makes of cars. *How much a month? Including room and board? How much for overtime?* Then you might ask what province she was from. You never asked her name. . . . To have a true friend inside the factory was not easy. Girls slept twelve to a room, and in the tight confines of the dorm it was better to keep your secrets. Some girls joined the factory with borrowed ID cards and never told anyone their real names.[5]

Influence of the Communist Party

Whether in school or working at a first job, young people in China live much like youths the world over. Their focus is on family; friends; dating; hobbies; popular culture, including films, music, and video games; and other ordinary concerns. Yet their daily lives also reflect the influence of the Communist Party. Although the party's rule is less oppressive than in the past, there are still restrictions on what young people can say and do. The national government restricts access to the Internet, freedom of the press, freedom of assembly, freedom to form organizations, and freedom of religion.

The Communist Party, which has more than 80 million members, dominates all aspects of China's political system. The party formed in 1921 and rose to power in 1949, when Mao Zedong's Marxist rebel armies defeated the Nationalists. The Communists set up the National People's Congress as the nation's highest political authority. That basic structure of government remains in place today, although with much greater autonomy on the local level. The general secretary of the Communist Party is the head of state. Local congresses modeled on the National People's Congress handle

Mao's Bloody History

For more than twenty years after the 1949 revolution, China had limited contact with the outside world. Communist leader Mao Zedong developed his own brand of Marxist thought—called Maoism—adapted to China's situation. He and his Communist cadres stripped landlords of ownership and redistributed farmland to the peasants who worked it. The Communist government seized control of the economy and banned capitalism, in the process wiping out almost all foreign investment.

Mao instituted vast projects like the Great Leap Forward in 1958, which set out to collectivize rural labor, and the Cultural Revolution, a period of political upheaval that began in 1966 and continued until Mao's death in 1976. Attempts to reorder the rural economy according to Socialist aims failed miserably and resulted in millions of deaths due to famine. Malnutrition led to birthrates that were cut almost in half. Mao's fanatical Red Guards carried out a political war to uncover supposed enemies among the Chinese people, an effort that brought about slaughter on a grand scale. In all, Mao's policies caused an estimated 70 million deaths in China. Yet Chinese textbooks censor this history, and young people are more focused on the present. "It's like this is near to me," a Chinese man in his midtwenties remarks about Mao's legacy, "but it's still history, it's not something I experienced. It's fifty years ago, but might as well have been a hundred or two hundred years ago."

Quoted in Alec Ash, "China's Youth: Do They Dare to Care About Politics?," *Dissent*, Spring 2013. www.dissentmagazine.org.

local affairs. Voters choose the members of the local congress, who in turn elect members to the national body. The Communist Party plays a major role in selecting candidates for these groups. Although eight minor parties aligned with the Communists can nominate candidates, no one is elected without ultimate support of the Communist Party. Chinese people can vote at age eighteen, but citizens vote only in local elections and basically have no voice in decisions made at the national level.

Although the Communist Party maintains rigid control over political freedoms in China, it has allowed remarkable changes in the national economy. Deng Xiaoping, a colleague of Mao who rose to become leader of China in 1978, pursued a program of economic reform that included many non-Marxist market-oriented ideas. These changes resulted in a burst of productivity that lifted millions of Chinese families out of poverty. Deng established strong relations with political and economic leaders in the United States and Europe. However, economic freedom and prosperity led young Chinese people to seek political freedom as well. In 1989 protests in favor of democracy attracted thousands of Chinese youths to Tiananmen Square in Beijing. On June 4 Deng's troops opened fire on the demonstrators, killing at least several hundred. Since Tiananmen, China's leaders have been quick to address any prodemocracy movements that might threaten Communist control. Discussion about Tiananmen remains a sore spot for the government. "From time to time an official Chinese spokesperson says, usually responding to a journalist, that this issue [about the Tiananmen massacre] was settled years ago," says Richard Rigby, head of the China Institute at the Australian National University. "It hasn't. If this were the case, the date would not be as sensitive as it is."[6] The government annually places Tiananmen under tight security on the anniversary of the massacre. Web-based searches about Tiananmen are blocked in China year round.

Some young Chinese people continue to hope for democratic reform. They see a government that is too timid to change. "[Communist leaders in China] seem to hold the opinion that if they don't change then they are safe," says Lily Han, a student in China. "I have to say that they don't think Chinese citizens have [the] ability to govern their own country. They are too scared to let citizens make decisions."[7] Nonetheless, most young people in China take one-party rule for granted, having grown up knowing no other system. It was their parents' and grandparents' generations that became embroiled in protests for democracy. Ordinary youths mostly accept the Communist precepts they learn in school and take pride in their country's rising status in world affairs. Yet they also overwhelmingly support capitalism and globalization of trade. They are more worried about inflation, inequality, and corruption than political freedoms.

> "[Communist leaders in China] are too scared to let citizens make decisions."[7]
>
> —Lily Han, a student in China

Concern About Getting Ahead

While politics does interest many young Chinese people, they are generally more concerned with doing well in school and getting ahead in a very competitive society. The vast majority grew up as the only child in the family, receiving a shower of parental attention—some would say a bit too much. In a society that for centuries has emphasized the collective good, they see new paths to individual prosperity. They think of themselves not just as workers but consumers. Like millennials around the world, they take for granted new technologies that are changing every aspect of daily life. They are a generation in a hurry, filled with expectations of wealth and success. "It was also the first generation in recent decades to experience a degree of personal choice in matters of career or love," says Howard W. French, an American expert on China, "and the first to have disposable income—or, for that matter, to have much of anything in Chinese stores to spend it on. Yet they are also under relentless pressure to get ahead."[8] It is this grinding pressure to succeed, beginning in school and continuing into the working years, that is most characteristic of the lives of Chinese youth today.

CHAPTER TWO

Family Life

Twenty-three-year-old Li Xue is an energetic young woman who lives with her parents in a cramped apartment in Beijing. Li has a quick mind, loves to read, and would like nothing better than to study law at a major university. Until recently, however, Li has had one major problem: Officially, she did not exist. When Li was born, her parents already had a five-year-old daughter, placing them in violation of China's one-child policy. Her mother's attempts to register Li at the local police station met with bureaucratic objections. A letter of approval for Li's birth was required, along with payment of a 5,000-yuan ($800) fine—a hefty sum Li's parents could not afford. As a result, Li was denied her Hukou, or household registration documents, which entitle citizens to education and health care.

Li has never spent a single day in school. She learned to read at home and made use of her sister's library card to check out books. Li's mother recalls how the child would cry at the sight of other children heading off to school. "She wanted to study at school, but she can't," says her mother, Bai Xiuling, a former factory worker. "My child has already missed the nine-year compulsory education. No money can buy her time back."[9] Without proper documents, Li could not apply for a job, get married, or even buy train tickets. In 2015 the Chinese government finally dropped the one-child policy. At last Li was able to secure an official paper establishing her identity. She welcomes this proof that she exists and is anxious to take her rightful place in society. Nonetheless, Li also wonders if the government will do anything to help her make up for all those lost years. More than 13 million formerly unregistered children in China are facing the same question.

Strong Family Bonds

The social upheaval caused by China's one-child policy shows how issues related to the family are crucial to the Chinese people. The bonds of the family are sacred in China. The family unit, and not the individual, is considered most important to society—an attitude that the ruling Communist Party certainly stresses. Family lines are traced back proudly over decades and sometimes centuries. François de Martrin-Donos, an industrial designer who lives in China, explains:

> The [alphabetic] character for family . . . is composed by two key elements: an upper part that represents a roof and a lower part which represents a pig (food). Therefore the family character traditionally represents a farm. . . . The farm is a place to rely on, but in return, needs to be maintained, including a set of responsibilities. In other words, "family" is the insurance of a stable life.[10]

The importance of the family in daily life also comes from Confucianism, an ancient philosophy that urges the virtues of what might be called loving teamwork. Every person is made to feel a special duty to the family. For example, if a family's shop is damaged in a storm, a dozen relatives are sure to show up the next day to help with the cleanup. Sons are expected not only to continue the family line but also to provide for their parents in their later years.

Most urban families in China today live in close quarters in overpriced apartments. Traditionally, three or even four generations lived together in the same household—although for reasons of space this practice is less frequent in cities today. Children are taught to be respectful of their elders and to do what they are told. The father is the head of the household, the main breadwinner (even when his wife also works), and the disciplinarian. He is expected to be reliable and trustworthy, if a trifle distant. It is

"In other words, 'family' is the insurance of a stable life."[10]

—François de Martrin-Donos, an industrial designer who lives in China

The bonds of the family are sacred in China. The family unit, and not the individual, is considered most important to society. Family lines are proudly traced back decades and even centuries.

usually the mother who runs the home, even when she too has a job. In cases of divorce, children typically live with their mother.

A child learns a specific way to address each member of the family, from aunts and uncles to older and younger siblings. While all relatives are addressed with respect, a greater deference is paid to older family members. For example, the father's elder brother (*bo fu*) is due slightly more respect than the younger brother (*shu fu*). Family members on the mother's side are addressed with terms that begin with the character *Wai* for "outside." This comes from the old male-dominant notion that women marrying into a new family remained outsiders. The Chinese system of specific names for relatives—used in addition to the person's given name—also helps avoid confusion in large extended families.

Respect for Elders

The most typical family structure in China is four-two-one: four grandparents, two parents, and one child. Young people in China reserve great respect for the wisdom of grandparents. In modern China, whether grandparents live in their children's household or in their own apartment, they spend as much time with their grandchildren as possible. Couples who both work may have a grandparent come over to mind their toddler during the day in lieu of day care. Studies have shown that Chinese grandparents tend to spoil their grandchildren with snacks such as chicken nuggets and doughnuts. This has raised concerns about childhood obesity. But most elders just want their grandkids—affectionately called little emperors and empresses—to enjoy the things that were not available in the days before the economic boom. "[The older] generation generally knows what it means to be hungry, not have a lot of choices and be deprived," notes market analyst Paul French. "Naturally they are delighted that their grandchildren . . . will grow up in a country so radically different than anything their grandparents could have visualized in the 1970s, 1980s, or even 1990s."[11]

Reverence for elders leads many young Chinese to return the favor and care for older family members as they decline in health. When a grandparent dies, she or he is honored in the family home with an ancestor altar that includes photographs, portraits, candles, and favorite personal items. Usually the altar is taken down after forty-nine days. Afterward the deceased is added to the family's ritual of ancestor worship. "What it typically involves is the preparation of food, incense and paper money as offerings to ancestors," says one Chinese youth in an online forum. "As to the spiritual aspect, well, to each his own. There isn't really a doctrine."[12]

> "Naturally they are delighted that their grandchildren . . . will grow up in a country so radically different than anything their grandparents could have visualized in the 1970s, 1980s, or even 1990s."[11]
>
> —Market analyst Paul French

Family Life in the City

Most young Chinese in large cities grow up in high-rise apartment blocks. To deal with the massive movement of people from rural to urban areas, the Chinese government has overseen construction of row after row of apartment buildings. Apartments tend to be small, plain, and expensive. A typical apartment in Beijing consists of a small living room, one or two bedrooms, a kitchen, and a bathroom. Older properties often share a bathroom in an outside hallway. A balcony provides access to the open air. Sometimes residents must outfit the apartment themselves with basic features such as cupboards, bathroom fixtures, wallpaper, and tile flooring. Elevators operate only now and then. To save money, a family on a modest income may refrain from turning on the central heat until late November. A couple with grandparents and two children can find apartment living to be a crowded experience. Yet Chinese are used to getting by with a minimum of personal space.

Wealthier Chinese can afford roomier apartments or stylish houses in the suburbs. A survey by Peking University found that the living space for an average Chinese family was 1,076 square feet (100 sq. m). The survey also showed that more than 87 percent of Chinese families owned or partially owned residential property.

Whether an apartment or single-family house, the entrance is typically lower than the rest of the home. Children and adults step up into the home or apartment. This goes back to the days when rural houses in China were raised above the ground for ventilation. Often family members or visitors remove their shoes before entering the living space. This helps keep the home clean and emphasizes that the family living space is special. "Honestly, the real question is why anyone wouldn't [remove shoes]," says Jennifer Hu in an online post. "It's the only sensible thing to do. What possible benefit could there be to tracking in dirt and mud into your house, especially if you have carpet? . . . Do you really want your mom to vacuum every day?"[13] Families may keep a rack for shoes in the vestibule and don light slippers once inside. Many Chinese people, both young and old, go barefoot inside the home.

Chinese homes usually do not have electric clothes dryers, although they do have washing machines. Youths in China grow up with laundry hanging on the balcony or all over the house or apartment, a comforting sign to them of an active family. Apart-

Moving Out of the Family Home

In some countries recent economic troubles have led to millennials living with their parents beyond their school years. However, China has seen an opposite trend, with young people moving out to lead separate lives. Traditionally, young Chinese have continued to live with their parents until they get married. But social changes have delayed thoughts of marriage for many millennials. Ambitious young people are seeking jobs in provinces far from their family home. Females are taking advantage of job opportunities that scarcely existed a decade ago. As they focus on careers, young adults may pursue an independent lifestyle that fits with their work routine. Nevertheless, family ties still exert a strong influence on Chinese youths. Sarah Zhao, a white-collar worker in Shanghai, explains:

> Many times when a Chinese child or young adult is preparing to make an important decision about their future, they will often take into consideration the feelings of their parents and their responsibility to their family. So in many respects the "family" plays a large role in influencing a person's decisions, even going so far as to cause an individual to sacrifice their own aspirations and goals to satisfy the needs of the family.

Quoted in Sean Upton-McLaughlin, "The Significance of Family in China," China Culture Corner, June 21, 2013. https://chinaculturecorner.com.

ment dwellers in Shanghai dry their clothes outside on a system of long bamboo poles. Air drying also saves money for families on a tight budget. Chinese households seldom have an electric oven for baking, although microwave ovens are increasingly common. Steaming, frying, and boiling are the preferred cooking methods.

Mealtime Habits

Meals are extremely important in a Chinese home. The dinner table is the focal point for a good deal of family life. One example of the preoccupation with food is the casual greeting, "Have you eaten already?"[14]—which goes back to the time when food was scarce in parts of China. For breakfast, a schoolchild will eat a dumpling, a bowl of sweet congee (rice porridge), and a steamed bun or fried dough stick. "One spoon congee, followed by one bite of fried dough stick," recalls Min, a young Chinese woman, about her childhood breakfasts. "You can even hear the cracking sound from the crispy stick before it gets melted by the soft rice. Yummy."[15] Usually, breakfast is eaten quickly at the table or on the run.

Dinner is more elaborate, with the family gathered together. Food is traditionally served from a common dish in the center of a round table, instead of on individual plates. Family members plunge into the central serving dish and whisk the food straight to their mouths. But when there are visitors, family members are expected to politely use their chopsticks to transfer chunks of meat, fish, and vegetables to a bowl of rice in front of them. The meal is carried on mostly in silence, with only a bit of conversation.

Dinner in China is served in courses. First comes a variety of dishes with marinated meat (usually pork or chicken), fish, and

Meals are extremely important in a Chinese home. Family members generally eat directly from common dishes in the center of a round table.

fresh vegetables from the local food market. Dishes are stir-fried, not deep fried, so the cooking is not greasy. There is no cheese, butter, or cream in traditional Chinese cooking either. After the main dishes comes a serving of noodle soup or pork meatball soup with sea kelp. A Chinese family will drink tea instead of coffee, and fruit is sufficient for a light dessert. As the meal progresses, the table becomes a tangle of arms and elbows as everyone reaches across his or her neighbor, tries food from each other's bowl, and passes around a favorite dish. Children become skillful with chopsticks, rapidly scooping mouthfuls of rice with the bowl held close to the chin. The air is filled with delicious smells and the sound of happy voices.

Emphasis on Work and Discipline

Helping in the kitchen and setting the table are two chores that many Chinese children are required to do. At an early age, a child might also learn to sort clothes into shirts, pants, and socks and to fold laundry neatly. Children help sweep the floors and pick up in the living room. A Chinese mother will take time to help younger children learn to do unfamiliar tasks. Occasionally, children save up their chores and complete them on Saturday when their schoolwork is done. While some Chinese households allow an only child to avoid housework in favor of watching television or playing video games, most parents assign chores as a way of enforcing good work habits and discipline.

Parents in China can be blunt in criticizing their children. They hold them to high standards to prepare them for the harsh competition of Chinese society. They also stress effort over innate ability. Whether solving math problems, learning to play the violin, or practicing gymnastics, a child is expected to outwork his or her rivals. To enforce this work ethic, some parents badger their children without letup. Although this type of parenting can lead a child to become successful, it can also breed resentment. "All because you fed me, housed me or 'cared' for me doesn't mean you are a parent," writes one Chinese teenager in an online forum. "Being a parent involves love, compassion and understanding. Prison inmates can get housing, food and care. It's the things from the heart that mean the most."[16]

> "Being a parent involves love, compassion and understanding. . . . It's the things from the heart that mean the most."[16]
>
> —A Chinese teenager writing in an online forum

27

Impact of the One-Child Policy

The one-child policy has enabled families in China to focus on achieving success for a single child. This smothering attention can be a burden. Many only children in China are left feeling lonely and isolated. Some research suggests that an only child is more likely to have trouble making friends. They might cope by creating imaginary friends or immersing themselves in hobbies. Others, however, enjoy the situation. Jessica, a twenty-three-year-old woman born in Weihai, in eastern Shandong Province, has few regrets about growing up as an only child:

> It is true that when both of my parents went to work, I ended up spending a lot of time alone at home and that might be one of the reasons that I am more of an introvert. But I am extremely lucky to have been born in an era of economic boom in China, so that my parents could let me try out different extracurricular activities, and ultimately send me to the US to study. You could argue that I am being a typically selfish only child, or that I just don't understand how having siblings really works, but I loved being the center of attention.[17]

The one-child policy also led Chinese couples to take drastic measures to end up with a male child, the preference in traditional Chinese culture. Many pregnant women underwent genetic testing to determine gender, and some couples resorted to abortion to avoid having a female child. Many families placed infant girls in orphanages, where they were raised without being aware of their roots or were offered for adoption to couples in other countries. Jessica's experience is typical of girls born under the one-child policy. "When I was born, my grandmother was so disappointed by my gender that she offered to hide me in the countryside so my parents could try for a boy," she says. "I only saw her again the

"When I was born, my grandmother was so disappointed by my gender that she offered to hide me in the countryside so my parents could try for a boy."[18]

—Jessica, a twenty-three-year-old woman born in Weihai

day before she died. The last thing she said to my dad was: at least adopt a son."[18] The result of such attitudes is that China now has many more young men than young women. Millions of young males will never find spouses inside their own country.

Family Life in Rural China

The one-child policy was enforced differently for families in rural China. In 1984 rural couples were allowed to have a second child if the first child was female or disabled—another example of the political and cultural bias against females in China. Local tradition

A family transports crops to their village on a country road. Life in rural China is often governed by crops and harvest season.

insisted that male children were needed to work the land and help with daily chores.

In rural areas most families live in wooden houses squeezed close together in small villages. The houses are larger than most city apartments, with several rooms and a courtyard. Many houses have an outdoor kitchen and no toilet, shower, or central heat. Water must be fetched from a pipe in the courtyard. More prosperous families may have indoor plumbing, a washing machine, and more than one television.

Life in the countryside is governed by the seasons. Corn and wheat harvests are busy times for young and old alike, but life

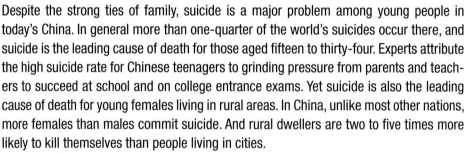

Suicide Among Young Females in Rural China

Despite the strong ties of family, suicide is a major problem among young people in today's China. In general more than one-quarter of the world's suicides occur there, and suicide is the leading cause of death for those aged fifteen to thirty-four. Experts attribute the high suicide rate for Chinese teenagers to grinding pressure from parents and teachers to succeed at school and on college entrance exams. Yet suicide is also the leading cause of death for young females living in rural areas. In China, unlike most other nations, more females than males commit suicide. And rural dwellers are two to five times more likely to kill themselves than people living in cities.

The reasons for the high suicide rate among young rural females are varied. A teenaged girl in a farming community often gets married very young, forgoing education for the lure of family. Yet her new family, including husband and mother-in-law, treats her like an outsider, leaving her feeling isolated and desperate. Moreover, rural life calls for hard labor day after day, whether in the fields or small factories. Lacking support at home, young females can become hopeless and develop mental health issues. An impulsive moment can lead to disaster. Many young females in rural China commit suicide by ingesting farm chemicals or pesticides. According to Xie Lihua, founder of the Cultural Development Center for Rural Women, "Suicide is seen as the way to solve problems in China."

Quoted in Yuan Ren, "Young Chinese Women Are Committing Suicide at a Terrifying Rate—Here's Why," *Telegraph* (London), October 20, 2016, www.telegraph.co.uk.

proceeds at a slower pace otherwise. After a dinner of home-grown vegetables, eggs, and fruit, the children follow their parents outside to the village square to play games and trade stories with their friends under the streetlights. Every ten days or so there is a local market, where neighbors gather to sell produce and buy household items, including toys for the youngsters. In general the selection is limited. "The infrastructure is nothing like what it is in cities," says Linka, a young Chinese blogger. "In rural China, the only goods you can find [are] from the most popular brand of that area and they are only sold in a family-owned grocery store."[19] Village life in China has proceeded unchanged like this for decades, but today young people increasingly are migrating to large cities like Shenzhen and Shanghai for better job opportunities.

CHAPTER THREE

School Life and Jobs

Each day at the Yongshi Primary School, one student is chosen to lead the class in performing eye exercises. For about ten minutes students massage different parts of their faces—forehead, bridge of the nose, eyebrows, and cheekbones. The exercises, which Chinese schoolchildren have been carrying out for decades, are based on ancient Chinese acupressure techniques. The Ministry of Education requires the exercises as a way to improve eye health and stave off myopia, or nearsightedness. Myopia, in which close objects are seen clearly but objects a few feet away appear blurry, is a growing problem among young Chinese. Rates of myopia have skyrocketed in recent years, with one study of high school students in Beijing finding that 80 percent were nearsighted.

Many experts question whether the eye exercises do any good. However, all agree that myopia is a serious problem for Chinese youths. Studies have linked nearsightedness to families who live in cities and have higher incomes and more education. Some vision researchers think the widespread myopia comes from children spending too much time indoors, hunched over books—or cell phones—and straining to see chalkboards. They say that healthy young eyes require natural sunlight, and they suggest forty-five minutes to an hour of daily outdoor play. Ian Morgan, a professor at the Zhongshan Ophthalmic Center in Guangzhou, also blames the constant pressure Chinese children are under to succeed. "It's not uncommon for children in China to study four hours a day at home on top of a full day of school as well as attend several hours of tutoring on weekends," he says. "Educational pressure and the disappearance of a strong preventive agent—time outdoors—is driving kids to myopia."[20]

The Chinese School System

Going to school in China is increasingly pressure packed and highly competitive. Children are taught at an early age that their performance in the classroom likely will determine their future success in life. A saying in Taoism, an ancient Chinese philosophy of patience and pious acceptance, declared that by doing nothing everything will be done. By contrast, today's schoolchildren learn that if every effort is not made, nothing important will be accomplished. The walls of their classrooms feature pictures of famous leaders like Mao Zedong and Zhou Enlai, the first premier of Communist China. Around their playing fields are signs that read "Education Changes Fate" and "Wisdom Leads You to Glory."[21] Their teachers stress the idea that education is not to be taken lightly. And it requires lots of hard work.

The education system in China is run by the state and is the largest in the world. Each student is entitled to a free education, provided he or she has the proper Hukou documents for the specific district. Parents must pay for books and school uniforms. All children begin school at age six and must attend for nine years. Preschool is available for children as young as two years old. It is more rigorous than day care, with a goal of teaching children discipline and how to work with a group. Primary school goes from grades one to six. Middle school, called junior secondary school, goes from grades seven to nine. High school, called senior secondary school, goes from grades ten to twelve and requires payment of entrance fees. College education is neither compulsory nor free in China. Applicants to universities face a great deal of competition for limited places.

The Chinese are proud of their school system. On standardized tests, students in China consistently outscore students from all other nations in core subjects such as math, reading, and science. Their success has led other countries to mimic the Chinese system's emphasis on memorization, rote learning, and preparing for tests. In China everything depends on strong performance in testing. In such a vast country, a sure method is needed to

"It's not uncommon for children in China to study four hours a day at home on top of a full day of school as well as attend several hours of tutoring on weekends."[20]

—Ian Morgan, a professor at the Zhongshan Ophthalmic Center in Guangzhou

A student enthusiastically raises his hand in a classroom in Baixiang County, China. School in China is very competitive, with children being taught at a young age that their performance in the classroom will determine their future success in life.

select the best students for higher education. "The students' schoolwork results do not just determine the students' future and destiny," notes one principal in Shanghai, "they also determine the success and failure of the teachers, the school and even the district's education standards."[22] Says a vice principal at another high school, "We love and hate exams. They increase our stress, yet they're the fairest."[23]

A School Day in China

To prepare for those all-important exams, Chinese students follow a strict routine. A grade-schooler rises early to be at school by 7:30 a.m. In large cities like Beijing and Shanghai, the school day ends early at 3:00 p.m., with only a short lunch break. This allows time for transportation by mass transit. However, in most places the school day extends to 4:00 or 5:00 p.m. Many schools also hold morning classes on Saturdays. Most primary school students in smaller communities get a lunch break of an hour or more. Some walk home to eat lunch and take a short nap. After school even young children must attend to homework before doing other things.

Public schools are very large, with thousands of students and several classes of forty or fifty at each grade level. Pupils gather on the school grounds at 7:30 as the loudspeakers buzz to life with music. While the national anthem plays and selected students raise the flag, younger children stand at attention. Older children march in place, wearing the bright red kerchiefs of the Young Pioneers, the youth group of the Communist Party. Chinese pupils must wait until the second grade to become a Young Pioneer. Each member pledges to work hard and devote all possible strength to the cause of communism. After the flag raising, students perform several minutes of calisthenics.

In cold weather students and teachers both wear heavy coats and gloves during the morning ceremony. Since most schools lack air-conditioning and heating, students usually leave their coats on all day in winter. Some schools are so cold that the students' breaths are visible in little clouds. Classrooms tend to be sparsely furnished, with only desks, chairs, a chalkboard, and a Chinese flag in the corner. There are no bulletin boards and few displays of artwork. Some rooms might have a propaganda poster with a slogan in block letters. Schools stress group activities, discipline, and obedience over individual expression.

In grade school each class has a class monitor, homework monitor, hygiene monitor, and politeness monitor. The politeness monitor reports to the teacher on students caught fighting

> "We love and hate exams. They increase our stress, yet they're the fairest."[23]
>
> —A vice principal at a Chinese high school

or cursing. Classroom elections are held for each position, with class monitor the most coveted office. Students mount their own campaigns, some mocking their opponents with biting insults and others asking humbly for votes. "It's an ugly campaign season, a mix of talent show, debate, old-fashioned politicking and dirty tricks," says Philip Kennicott, an American reporter. "It's part 'American Idol,' part 'Survivor.'"[24]

Teachers and Teaching Methods

Teachers in China generally are all business, and they demand respect. "The relationship between students and instructors determines the classroom environment," says Echo Lu, who went to public school in China before moving to the United States. "In China, teaching in the classroom is the most respected career. Students are trained to 100% obey their instructors."[25] Most teachers employ a chalk-and-talk strategy, briskly writing on the chalkboard and lecturing while the children race to take down the words in their notebooks. There is little interaction between the teacher and individual students—one result of having such large classes. When asked a question, students must raise their hands and be chosen to answer. Students stand beside their desks to recite or to respond to a question and never speak out of turn. To show respect, they refer to their teacher in writing as "Our dear teacher."[26] Assignments, written on paper so thin it can almost be seen through, are submitted ceremoniously at the teacher's desk with a bow.

Students in primary school study math, geography, Chinese, and natural science. In third grade they begin to learn English. Primary school students also receive instruction in painting, music, physical education, and moral thought. The latter includes small amounts of history and political science mixed with stories of past Chinese heroes. Schools in China stress rote learning and memorization over critical-thinking skills. On tests, students are expected to reproduce the facts they have learned exactly as they have learned them. In a *New Yorker* article about modern life in China, writer Peter Hessler describes one child's primary school education:

> Everything revolves around repetition and memorization, which works beautifully for math. But other subjects often devolve into scattered facts that career between tradition-

al and modern, Chinese and foreign. I was amazed by the stuff [Chinese pupil] Wei Kia learned—the most incredible assortment of de-systematized knowledge that had ever been crammed into a child.[27]

Teachers assign mountains of homework, even on holidays. They work hard just like their students, often correcting papers while the class is completing an assignment. At the end of every term, primary students each receive a report card of thirty pages. It features measurements of the student's height, weight, eyesight, and lung capacity, as well as the teacher's evaluation. One page includes blank circles above comments like *pushes him/ herself to succeed* and *enjoys the fruits of hard work*. The student is supposed to fill in each circle with a smiley face or frowning face to evaluate his or her own performance.

A teacher addresses his class in Chengdu, China. Teaching is one of the most respected careers in China. Students must obey the teacher and can speak only if they are given permission.

Middle School and High School

The first major test Chinese students face is the exam to get into a top middle school. Failure at this level can reduce the chance of reaching a good high school or going to college at all. Fifth-grade students take a test-prep class in addition to their regular classes and study for the middle school exam at every opportunity. Many children continue with music lessons and instruction in English, art, and computer science at the same time. Parents whose child is on the borderline academically invest in these activities to help sway school officials. Some parents even make donations to a favored middle school of up to $1,000.

In middle school a student's workload continues to increase. Students arrive at 7:00 a.m. to do extra reading and reciting in English or Chinese. The regular school day goes until 5:00 p.m., with physics, chemistry, biology, and political science added to the primary school subjects. After a short dinner break that includes playtime for exercise, students remain at school for tutoring sessions or study halls.

Ninth graders again must succeed on a crucial test to attend a leading high school. Once accepted, students face an even more grueling schedule. Many high schools require students to live on campus in dorms, where juniors live eight to a room and seniors four to a room. Devices such as cell phones, computers, and even hair dryers are forbidden. Students rise early to join their teacher for a reading session in Chinese or English. Five students in each class are exempt so they can mop the classroom floors and help clean the campus. Daily classes run until 5:45 p.m. There is a midmorning session for flag raising and regimented exercise in a nearby field or stadium. Students also get a short break for lunch and dinner. At 6:30 p.m. students return to the classroom for more study or to work with a tutor. Not until 11:00 p.m. do weary students make it back to the dorm. Classes also are held on Saturdays until almost 5:00 p.m. "Lack of sleep is very common for Chinese high-school students,"[28] notes Yao Zhang, a Chinese native with a PhD in economics and education from Columbia University.

> "Lack of sleep is very common for Chinese high-school students."[28]
>
> —Yao Zhang, a Chinese native with a PhD in economics and education from Columbia University

Crisis for Rural Schools in China

China's massive migration from rural areas to cities has left village schools struggling to survive. In 2001 the Chinese government announced a policy to shut down remote village schools and pool their resources to support schools in larger towns. From 2000 to 2015 almost three-quarters of all rural primary schools were closed, a total of more than three hundred thousand schools. Chinese children in many rural villages lack access to a quality school. Many are living with their grandparents while their parents seek jobs in the city. For village children, the nearest primary school often lies hours away, with no bus service available. A village teacher may try to hold classes for a handful of local students, but the school building is usually falling apart and the classroom lacks even basic resources. Besides giving lessons, the teacher must also serve as cook and caretaker. Government spending per student on rural schools averages less than half the amount spent in Beijing and other large cities.

When a village school shuts down, children are forced to enroll in a distant boarding school. Conditions are crowded and harsh, with bare concrete walls, windows with no curtains, and no central heating. Most boarding schools struggle to provide students with three meals a day. Children become resigned to a difficult future. Dropout rates are high. Less than 10 percent of rural students go on to attend senior high school.

Preparing for the Gaokao

Pressure to excel ratchets up to feverish levels during a student's high school years. Every student is focused on passing the dreaded two-day college entrance exam called the *gaokao* — often referred to as the toughest and most competitive in the world. The gaokao (the term means "big test" in Mandarin) determines whether a student is eligible for college as well as which college he or she can attend.

Ten million high school seniors take the exam each year in the first week of June. Only about 60 percent score high enough to make it into college at all, let alone gain acceptance to a prestigious university. Students are tested on knowledge in Chinese, mathematics, English, and one elective of the student's choice, either science or humanities. "A high or low mark determines life opportunities and earning potential," explains Alec Ash, a British correspondent. "That score is the most important number of any

Chinese child's life, the culmination of years of schooling, memorization and constant stress."[29] Zhao Xiang, a high school graduate from Guizhou Province, admits that the anxiety before the test can be overwhelming. "Sometimes it was pressure from my family, sometimes it was the expectations from my teacher, sometimes it was pressure from myself," he says. "I was constantly in a really bad mood in the period before the *gaokao*. I was really confused."[30]

The gaokao has become a public spectacle in China. Newspapers print sample questions to give readers a glimpse of the test. TV news reports warn about the use of earpieces, radio devices, and stashed answers to help test takers cheat. One story tells of a syndicate in Jiangxi Province that charges parents up to 1 million yuan (almost $150,000) to hire a professional test taker to pose as their child. During testing days in cities where the exam is administered, airlines reroute flights and nearby construction sites shut down. At the end of the second day, parents crowd the streets outside the hall waiting nervously for their children to appear. Many of the students emerge looking dazed and exhausted. Proud parents reward their efforts with bouquets of flowers and pose with them for cell phone pictures. It will be a month or more before the results are known, but most students are simply relieved that the ordeal is over. The word *gaokao* has been a spur and a warning for them since grade school. Katherine Liu, who was able to pass the test several years ago, admits, "I survived the *gaokao*, although those exams torture me in my sleep to this day."[31]

> "That score [on the gaokao] is the most important number of any Chinese child's life, the culmination of years of schooling, memorization and constant stress."[29]
>
> —Alec Ash, a British correspondent in China

College Life

For Chinese students who qualify, college life can seem like a well-earned breather after years of toil and anxiety. However, the average university still requires a great deal of hard work. Aside from attending classes, each student must attend a monitored study hall between 6:00 and 10:00 p.m. each weekday. Students select a major when they enter college and are expected to fol-

Chinese parents wait anxiously outside a high school while their children take the 2017 college entrance exam, known as gaokao. The rigorous two-day exam determines whether a student is eligible for college, as well as which college he or she can attend.

low through on that major. Changing majors is a long, tedious process designed to discourage second thoughts. Students go to classes with a registered unit, which means they see the same group of students every day throughout their college years. Often members of a unit become close friends and colleagues in their chosen discipline for life.

Students must live in the dorms throughout their college careers. A typical room houses four to six students, with men and women in separate dorms. Privacy is limited, but as roommates become acquainted they share late-night stories, play cards, and banter like college students everywhere. Since universities tend to be located in larger cities, roommates also use mass transit to have a night on the town. This might include hanging out at a restaurant or bar, singing karaoke, or seeing a movie. "For most Chinese students, going to a university is probably the first time we interact with people from other provinces," says Ruoyu Liu, a student at Sun Yat-sen University in Guangzhou. "As Chinese has a lot of distinctive languages/dialects, the best ice breaker would be teaching others how to insult someone in your native dialect—yes, you would learn a lot of coarse words after 4 years. Really fun experience."[32]

Job Outlook for Young Chinese

For college graduates in China, the employment picture can look murky. The slowest economic growth in a generation has young job seekers on edge. Many are looking for their first jobs, having never had time for even part-time employment during their hectic school days. And large numbers of college graduates are pouring into the job market each year. In 2015 more than 7.5 million new graduates sought jobs in China. Dang Lirong, a twenty-two-year-old trained nurse, is all too typical. After a year interning at a Beijing hospital, she now combs through jobs fair listings, looking for something in the medical field. "I didn't know it would be like this," she says. "I took the major because I thought it would give me a good job."[33]

Economists point to a mismatch between what Chinese graduates want to do and the actual jobs available. Companies demand salespeople, agents, technicians, service staff, and waiters, while young Chinese people would rather become attorneys, teachers, administrators, accountants, and human resource managers. Ma Chao, a mechanics major, knows he could get a job in sales, but he resists. "I'm not really cut out for that," he says. "There are jobs out there, but few meet my expectations."[34] As a result, many Chinese youths are becoming so-called boomerang kids, returning home to live with their parents while they contemplate the future.

One irony in China today is that the more educated an individual is, the harder it is to find a job. The unemployment rate for college graduates is slightly greater than for those who did not finish high school. At the same time, the salary gap between the average twenty-two-year-old graduate and an assembly-line

A Cram School in Maotanchang

Students come from miles around to study at the special high school in Maotanchang, an isolated town in the foothills of Anhui Province in eastern China. More than twenty thousand students, most from rural villages, attend Maotanchang's so-called cram school, a prep-test center that gets them ready for the gaokao college entrance exam. They enter and leave the school grounds in hordes, many dressed in black-and-white windbreakers with the English slogan "I believe, I can do it." The high school specializes in training these earnest young men and women to be test-taking machines. Yang Wei, the hardworking son of a peach farmer, knows that passing the gaokao is his ticket to a bright future. "If you connected all of the practice tests I've taken over the past three years," he says, "they would wrap all the way around the world."

To further the school's mission, administrators and town elders in Maotanchang try to eliminate all distractions. Dorm rooms are tiny and lack electrical outlets. Cell phones and laptop computers are banned. Romantic encounters between students are not just frowned upon but forbidden. The town itself has no billiards hall, no video arcade, and no Internet café. The school's all-male teaching staff maintains military-style discipline, while security guards roam the campus in golf carts looking for straying students. All focus is on achieving the minimum gaokao score necessary to enter a college. As Yang admits, "There's nothing to do but study."

Quoted in Brook Larmer, "Inside a Chinese Test-Prep Factory," *New York Times Magazine*, December 31, 2014. www.nytimes.com.

worker of the same age is shrinking. Average monthly wages for line workers rose by almost 10 percent from 2013 to 2014, while average monthly wages for college graduates increased by only about 7 percent. As incentive for recent graduates, the State Council, China's national governing body, has set up programs to help them start their own small businesses. The programs include tax relief, cheap business loans, and government subsidies for employee benefits. Yet there have been few takers. Experts note that many graduates sit at home in front of a computer and dream of launching a billion-dollar start-up such as Taobao, the Chinese equivalent to the auction site eBay, instead of pursuing more realistic goals. According to Guo Liqun, a recruitment director, "Many students have unreasonably high expectations for their jobs, contributing to this year's grim job prospects."[35]

CHAPTER FOUR

Social Life and Marriage

The West has its millennials—the Chinese have their *diaosi*. The word *diaosi* began as a crude slang term meaning "loser," but young Chinese today employ it as a half-joking badge of honor. Diaosi are young workers, both male and female, who are struggling to make their mark in a stagnant economy they feel is letting them down. They have jobs that do not pay enough and seem to lead nowhere. They spend hours online on social media, exchanging thoughts about work, life, the opposite sex, and popular culture.

These young people do not really consider themselves losers so much as world-weary observers in search of a lucky break. They are expert at making fun of themselves and the hopelessness of their situation. Diaosi are noted for being unmarried and rather clumsy in social situations and face-to-face encounters. Surveys of self-described diaosi have found that many have moved far from their hometowns in search of higher-paying jobs. Almost three-quarters of them send some of their wages home each month. Even those who find a bit of success continue to think of themselves as diaosi. "My base pay is 5000, including commission, I make 100K a year, yet I still feel like I am a *diaosi*," writes one young man on the popular news blog *chinaSMACK*. "With overwhelming stress, without a house or car, and not daring to buy a house or car, scrimping and saving where I can in my spending, so much that I even think I've developed clinical depression."[36]

Using Social Media
China's state-controlled media sees the whole diaosi culture, with its underlying criticism of the economy and government policies,

as a potential threat. The *People's Daily,* the official newspaper of the Chinese Communist Party, even published a biting editorial titled "The Belittling of Oneself, Can We Give It a Rest?" The writer claimed that the diaosi attitude is a danger to overall mental health. But others think the real problem lies with young people who are overworked and dizzy with stress. Since early childhood they have had to deal with crushing pressures to succeed from both parents and teachers. "There's almost no space for young people in China," says Lu-Hai Liang, who was born in China and raised in England. "The need to compete in the professional and marital marketplaces means young people need to focus on education and connections."[37]

Schoolwork leaves little time for socializing and relaxation for most young people in China. In this atmosphere using social media can be a welcome release. Like young people the world over, Chinese youths turn to their cell phones the moment they wake up. They check out texts from friends, play games for a few minutes, and consult the latest videos—quickly moving on to other sites if a video is not sufficiently interesting. Most are expert at getting the information they want with great speed. This talent comes from having to wedge their limited phone sessions into a busy schedule every day. (It also helps that Chinese websites tend to be extremely fast.) Some high schools ban cell phones outright as preparations for the college entrance exam intensify. At a school in Wuhan, a city in Hubei Province, teachers who catch a student hiding a cell phone confiscate it, smash it in front of the class, and put it on display as a warning to other students.

Chinese youths love their cell phones. A recent *Financial Times* survey found that 92 percent of those aged eighteen to thirty in China owned a smartphone. But their social media world is quite different from the one familiar to young people in most other nations. The Chinese government employs what its citizens call the Great Firewall. It blocks many social websites created in the West, including Facebook, Twitter, YouTube, Pinterest, Snapchat, Instagram, Blogspot, and Flickr. Certain well-known news

> "The need to compete in the professional and marital marketplaces means young people need to focus on education and connections."[37]
>
> —Lu-Hai Liang, who was born in China and raised in England

Commuters stare at their smartphones as they ride the train in Hong Kong. It is estimated that 92 percent of eighteen- to thirty-year-olds in China own a smartphone.

sites such as the *New York Times*, the *Wall Street Journal*, Reuters, and *Le Monde* also are blocked, as well as newer additions such as Google News. Websites generally are blocked because they refuse to comply with Chinese censorship laws. The state fears the political fallout from allowing too much online freedom. Protesters would have the means to organize last-minute flash mob rallies. As Joseph Wang, a research scientist, notes, "The thing about facebook, twitter, and youtube is that you can tell 100,000 to show up on location X on date Y, and you can form a social group pretty quickly."[38] Young cyberbuffs can get around the system by hooking up to a virtual private network, which can evade the Great Firewall and connect to blocked sites. However, the government is constantly on guard against these networks, blocking their servers and choking off their bandwidth.

Homegrown Social Media Sites

The Chinese government also wants to protect homegrown Internet companies from outside competition. As a result, young Chinese use their own social media sites. Several have met with huge success, garnering millions of users. WeChat, a mobile app that stands in for Facebook Messenger, is likely the largest communication hub in China. Sina Weibo serves as a combination blogging site and Chinese version of Twitter. Its 140-character limit allows for more detailed messages, since each Mandarin character is like a word and conveys more content than an English letter. Chinese youths flock to Youku Tudou to watch videos and download both foreign and domestic movies. Dian-Ping features users' reviews of restaurants and stores and also offers discount coupons for merchandise. Like the other major social media sites, its appeal to the young has rocketed its value into the billions.

Cell phones and social networking can become time-wasting obsessions. But they also have many positive effects on youths in China. One benefit is to help them organize their hectic lives. Social calendar apps send reminders about family events. A busy student can at least send an e-card for her favorite aunt's birthday. Teens can consult news sites to get some idea of what is happening in the world outside their school and social group. A self-absorbed diaosi, having grown up as a pampered only child, can use social networks to break out of his or her shell and interact with a large group of friends for the first time.

> "The thing about facebook, twitter, and youtube is that you can tell 100,000 to show up on location X on date Y, and you can form a social group pretty quickly."[38]
>
> —Joseph Wang, a research scientist in China

Leisure Activities

To a Western observer the daily life of a teenager in China can seem overly structured and even monotonous. One visitor from France described a typical day this way:

Get up at 6 am, eat noodles, go to school, do some gym, attend class, eat rice and fried chicken, drink tea with milk, chat on the phone, share and comment [on] stuff online, attend more classes, watch movies on your phone, go to granny's place, do homework, send and share more stuff on your phone, have some rehearsal and extra classes like math or piano, watch stuff online, sleep.[39]

Young Chinese in cities actually spend their limited leisure time doing many of the same things as young people elsewhere in the developed world. They meet friends at the shopping mall and hang out together or take in a movie. Girls especially love to drift into different stores, try on outfits, and haggle over prices. The Chinese have a term—*ren shan ren hai*, or "people mountain people sea"—for the crowds of enthusiastic shoppers that descend on malls and city streets during holidays. Since only the wealthiest teens have cars, youths walk the streets and use public transit in the evenings. They gather nightly at teahouses, bars, and cafés. They love to sing karaoke and play pool, foosball, darts, and other games—often for money. Young office workers socialize with coworkers at restaurants and dance clubs. Traditionally, this is a means to develop *guanxi*, or business relationships built on trust. However, young Chinese workers today approach these after hours get-togethers simply as a way to relax and have fun.

Another popular form of relaxation is going to a park. With living space at a premium, the lure of wide-open acres is strong. Chinese parents take their children to soak up the sunshine and enjoy the outdoors. In Ritan Park in Beijing, rides for smaller kids such as bumper cars and a mini-train are crowded into a small enclosure for which an entry fee is charged. Even slides cost 10 yuan ($1.50) an hour to use, so most children end up playing tag or making up their own games for free. Teenagers kick a soccer ball, play badminton or table tennis, test the nimbleness of their feet with the Chinese version of hacky sack, fly kites, practice tai chi or other forms of martial arts, or lie on the grass and consult their smartphones. Some teens pursue an artistic hobby such as sketching or calligraphy. Many Chinese enjoy playing board games outdoors, including chess and mah-jongg. In large industrial cities

like Beijing, Baoding, and Chongqing, air pollution can spoil the idea of spending some healthy time outside. On certain days a thick gray haze settles over the city. Nonetheless, Chinese both young and old seem to take it in stride. Even on the worst days, few are seen wearing protective surgical masks.

Pop Culture and Music

Wherever Chinese teens go, they love to listen to music. Most of their favorite artists and groups come from outside China, especially Taiwan and South Korea. The repetitive choruses and odd lingo of Korean pop songs—called K-pop—exert a special fascination for many young Chinese. A number of pop groups in China

LGBT in China

Sun Bin knows the anguish of being bullied for his sexual orientation. From his first day in primary school, Sun faced harassment from classmates who called him a sissy and much worse names. A dozen female classmates once carried him into the girls' bathroom and dumped him inside. "I was scared and crying in the bathroom for hours," says Sun. "I felt hopeless and humiliated." Now 21, Sun has struggled with depression and more than once has attempted suicide. Not even his parents would accept the fact that he is gay. "They blamed me for not looking and acting like a 'normal boy,'" he recalls.

Sun's experience is all too typical for LGBT—lesbian, gay, bisexual, transsexual—individuals in China. In a recent online survey of LGBT youths in Guangzhou, 77 percent reported at least one instance of bullying at school due to their sexual orientation or gender identity. Forty-four percent reported incidents of verbal abuse and ridicule.

Despite this harassment, there are signs that attitudes are changing. The state ended sanctions against homosexual activity in 1997. Western-style Gay Pride parades and demonstrations in favor of LGBT rights are increasingly common in China. The Internet slang term *gao-ji,* meaning two people of the same sex having an affair, has become an accepted part of the media's vocabulary. Although gay marriage remains illegal, young same-sex couples occasionally stage public wedding ceremonies to highlight the issue. As elsewhere in the world, traditional beliefs and prejudices are being reexamined in today's China.

Quoted in Fan Yiying, "LGBT Youth Face Lots of Bullying, Little Acceptance," *Sixth Tone,* March 21, 2017, www.sixthtone.com.

model their songs and performance styles on Korean bands. Chinese bands lack the rebelliousness of rock music in the West. Government censorship often is cited as the reason. According to Yang Haisong, a punk musician in Beijing, "The youth culture in China was never mainstream, you can't even say it's a counterculture, in fact we have no youth culture, because everyone is subject to the media and external influences—they do not have their own point of view."[40] Many Chinese youth prefer the music of Western stars such as Adele, Lady Gaga, Justin Bieber, Taylor Swift, and Maroon 5.

Teenagers in China watch American TV shows obsessively. They not only enjoy the shows for entertainment but also use them to improve their English. The most popular Chinese productions on TV are war-themed dramas and martial arts fantasies. Youths enjoy romantic series that take a bittersweet look at high school life as well. For China's multitudes of single children, television and movies represent a welcome escape from the perils of social life. "We grew up alone," says a typical only child. "I like to watch movies on my PC, alone in my room, where I can cry if I want to."[41]

The Challenges of Dating

Dating can be a challenge for Chinese young people. Although attitudes toward dating are growing more relaxed in China's larger cities, most of the nation still follows the old courtship rituals. Males are expected to take the initiative in relationships, and parents' consent remains crucial in the selection of a mate for their son or daughter. To add to the difficulty, many parents discourage their children—particularly females—from dating in high school or during the first two years of college. Barbara Li, a twenty-year-old who works for a magazine in Shanghai, was one of these sheltered offspring. "I've been single all my life," she says. "In high school, we were not permitted to have boyfriends. At university there were only six boys in my class."[42]

Even with all the rapid changes in Chinese society, opportunities for dating still remain limited for many young adults. Women like Li increasingly turn to dating services. Matchmaking sites online have exploded in popularity. "The old family and social networks that people used to rely on for finding a husband or wife have fallen apart," observes James Farrer, an American sociologist who has studied dating and marriage in today's China. "There's a huge sense of dislocation in China, and young people don't know where to turn."[43]

Part of the problem relates to the one-child policy and its aftereffects. The policy created a huge gender imbalance in favor of male children—with 118 boys born for every 100 girls. Now millions of young men in China seek spouses in vain among the diminished pool of young females. And smart, accomplished young

> "We grew up alone. I like to watch movies on my PC, alone in my room, where I can cry if I want to."[41]
>
> —An only child in China

women are delaying marriage to focus on their careers. State media has begun to warn about the plight of these so-called leftover women who reach age thirty with no husband and no prospects. "There is lots written in the state media about how all these tens of millions of unmarried men pose a threat to society," says Leta Hong Fincher, an expert on gender inequality in China. "But at the other end of the spectrum, unmarried women who are not fulfilling their 'duty to the nation' by getting married and having children are also seen as a threat."[44]

Courtship

Typically, girls and boys get introduced and acquainted with each other only in group settings, with friends meeting for drinks or karaoke. At a dance club, males and females dance together in groups as well. When a couple begins to flirt or displays special rapport, the group will subtly find a way to give them some time alone. Disappearing for a walk together outside can be a momentous step for a new couple. However, even holding hands is generally out of bounds. Public displays of affection are rare among young Chinese. In addition, Chinese couples almost never exchange the words wo ai ni ("I love you"). "We said, 'wo xihuan ni,' ('I like you'), to express our deepest romantic feelings," says Kaiping Peng, a psychology professor at the University of California–Berkeley. "Before then, you just showed love through holding hands, kissing, or maybe writing or doing something nice—but you never said it."[45] On the other hand, dating couples in China often declare their devotion to each other in public by wearing matching outfits.

> "Unmarried women who are not fulfilling their 'duty to the nation' by getting married and having children are . . . seen as a threat."[44]
>
> —Leta Hong Fincher, an expert on gender inequality in China

Dating is not taken casually, since most Chinese do not "play the field" before marriage as in Western countries. Dating is often regarded as a form of courtship. If a girl tells her parents about the boy she is seeing, it means she is interested in a serious relationship. An invitation to meet her parents practically serves as an engagement. Should either set of parents disapprove of the match, the relationship is most likely doomed.

A young couple sits together in Dujiangyan, China. Dating is not taken casually in China and is often regarded as a form of courtship leading to marriage.

Sex before marriage has traditionally been frowned upon although, in sexual matters, men are expected to be more experienced than women. Even this is changing. Sex before marriage has become much more common in China, especially among Westernized youths in large cities.

Wedding Customs

When a couple decides to marry, they announce their intentions by hosting a dinner for family and friends at which they exchange rings. By tradition, the groom's family makes a series of gifts to the family of the bride. Cash gifts are arranged in amounts of nines (99, 999, etc.), since a homonym for the *nine* character in Mandarin means "forever." Wedding plans soon occupy the couple's every spare moment. Much thought goes into choosing the most auspicious date for the wedding. The young people seek out a fortune-teller, who in turn consults Chinese almanacs for the exact right day. These almanacs, sold on the street and

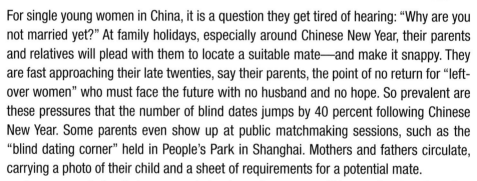

Pressure to Find a Spouse

For single young women in China, it is a question they get tired of hearing: "Why are you not married yet?" At family holidays, especially around Chinese New Year, their parents and relatives will plead with them to locate a suitable mate—and make it snappy. They are fast approaching their late twenties, say their parents, the point of no return for "leftover women" who must face the future with no husband and no hope. So prevalent are these pressures that the number of blind dates jumps by 40 percent following Chinese New Year. Some parents even show up at public matchmaking sessions, such as the "blind dating corner" held in People's Park in Shanghai. Mothers and fathers circulate, carrying a photo of their child and a sheet of requirements for a potential mate.

In response to family harassment about marriage, young Chinese often turn to online dating sites. These present opportunities for girls to narrow their search to precise specifications. They can choose their ideal husband's age, looks, residential area, education, and financial situation. A website like Baihe claims to have made thousands of successful matches. Baihe requires clients to give their real names and employs third-party firms to check out details about education and personal finances.

As for girls who are too busy to date, they can rent a fake boyfriend through Taobao, an e-commerce site. For a reasonable fee, a handsome escort will stay by a young lady's side throughout the most tedious family gatherings.

Quoted in Manya Koetse, "Online Dating in China: Serious Business," *What's On Weibo* (blog), June 5, 2015. www.whatsonweibo.com.

containing detailed predictions about different periods of the year, are considered a source of almost occult knowledge. However, tradition says it is bad luck for the bride and groom to do an almanac analysis of their own.

For the wedding ceremony, the bride wears a jacket and skirt of bright red, considered a joyous color. Over her face she wears a veil or a covering of beads. The groom typically wears a coat and tie, although some may don a traditional patterned robe. Many couples get married at the office of the Civil Affairs Bureau and reserve their celebration for a banquet afterward in a hall filled with flowers. There, guests bring gifts of money in red envelopes. A special fruit dish composed of dates, peanuts, longan (a tropical fruit), lotus seeds, and chestnuts is served to the bride and groom for good luck. Together these ingredients make up a homonym for a phrase that urges the couple to have a healthy child very soon. The reception banquet includes the usual spate of sentimental speeches and toasts. The married couple also visits each table in turn and toasts the guests. Some newlyweds embark on a honeymoon trip, but others prefer to plunge into their new marital routine as soon as possible. Relief at no longer having to endure their parents' constant prodding to get married, some couples say, feels almost as good as passing the gaokao.

CHAPTER FIVE

Holidays and Religious Life

Every year on November 11, young Chinese people take to their computers and smartphones for what began as a celebration of bachelorhood and consumerism. The celebration now includes both males and females. Online merchandisers of every sort offer their best bargains of the year. Discounts of 50 percent are commonplace. Singles' Day, as it is called, shows that a popular new holiday can be ginned up out of almost nothing—as long as it has the enthusiastic support of the young and the hip. So successful has Singles' Day become that it is now the world's largest online shopping event of the year. On Singles' Day in 2016, retailers on Alibaba, China's largest e-commerce site, racked up sales of more than $17.8 billion, outdoing the experts' predictions and smashing all previous records. And the celebration has expanded beyond the shopping angle. "As China's youth population steadily grows," explains Jessica Tang, a teacher in Beijing, "Singles Day continues to become more and more popular throughout the country with the introduction of a variety of activities to celebrate it. On this day, groups of single friends get together, go for a drink, chat, head to KTV [Karaoke TV, the Chinese slang term for karaoke bars] and shopping, and simply enjoy a fun time together."[46] Zhou Bokun, a young online shopper, says, "I won't call it a festival. But, it [does have] a festival atmosphere."[47]

Festival Days

In many ways Singles' Day is the perfect holiday for China's diaosi, its "beautiful losers." Supposedly, it began in 1993 when four students at Nanjing University decided to commemorate their bachelor status. They chose November 11 (11/11) because each *1* represents a smooth stick (*guang gun*), which also refers to a bachelor or single boy. The celebration caught on as a kind of anti-Valentine's Day for those who chronically lack romantic companionship. Young men would eat four dough sticks on November 11 to bring them better romantic luck next year. Corporations seized on Singles' Day as a way to boost online sales to unmarried urban youths. And, like Black Friday in the United States, the tradition caught on in a big way among both males and females.

Chinese workers sort parcels ordered online during Singles' Day. Every year on November 11, online merchandisers offer their best bargains for Singles' Day, and young Chinese take to their computers and smartphones to shop and celebrate bachelorhood and consumerism.

In a nation that is officially atheist, festivals and celebrations take the place of religious holidays. Atheism, which is part of Communist doctrine, rejects belief in God or a higher power in favor of materialist views that physical matter is all that exists. As a secular or nonreligious nation, the Chinese state does not outlaw religious practice but places it under certain restrictions. In any case, surveys indicate that the closest thing to widespread religious belief in China relates to Buddhism. About 30 percent of those surveyed admitted to following at least one Buddhist belief or practice. Buddhism is a philosophy of life based on the twenty-five-hundred-year-old teachings of Siddhartha Gotama, known as the Buddha. Followers are urged to lead a moral life by minding their thoughts and actions and to seek enlightenment or understanding. Chinese Buddhists go to a temple not to worship, but to pay respect to the image of the Buddha. To Chinese youths Buddhism mainly represents an age-old tradition of thought in China. Aside from Buddhists, religious-minded young Chinese, whether Christian, Muslim, or of some other faith, represent a small percentage of the overall population.

Secular festivals in China are notable for encouraging people to take part, to participate in planned activities, not just gather with family or friends. Many young people in China recall the sights, sounds, and smells of the festivals they attended in childhood and how much fun they had taking part in the colorful rituals. Although some of the more Westernized young Chinese people make a show of celebrating American or European holidays, many youths are content to take part in traditional Chinese festivals along with their elders. To them these special days represent more than just a break from school or work. "Sometimes, I think it's incorrect to say young people like holidays only because they can take a rest," says Wenzhe Chen on an online forum. "They are still children somehow. If they grow up, left their home, they would miss their families and try to get home in every spring festival."[48]

> "[Young Chinese] are still children somehow. If they grow up, left their home, they would miss their families and try to get home in every spring festival."[48]
>
> —Wenzhe Chen, a Chinese student

Taoism, a Mystical Religion

The Lantern Festival, among many other Chinese customs of today, bears aspects of Taoism, a religion and philosophy of life that dates back two thousand years. Followers seek the Tao, usually translated as "the way"—the ultimate principle of order and creativity in the universe. The Tao unifies a world filled with opposites, expressed as Yin and Yang. These include light and dark, heat and cold, activity and rest. Taoism is based on teachings attributed to Lao-tzu, a legendary philosopher who probably never existed. While the Tao itself is not a god, Taoism includes many deities that are worshipped in Taoist temples throughout China. Thus a visit to a Taoist temple has become a tradition during celebrations such as the Spring Festival.

Young Chinese, having grown up with Taoist teachings, continue to follow certain of its ideas. For example, many conduct daily exercises using the breathing and relaxation technique called qigong. This practice seeks to preserve health by allowing the qi, or life force, to flow freely through the body. Another Taoist concept is feng shui, which employs ideas of visual harmony to decorate homes and offices. "Taoism has spread its tentacles everywhere," says Li Yuanguo, an expert on religion at the Academy of Social Sciences in Chengdu. "It defines the relationships between individual humans, and between humankind and nature. That's still very relevant."

Quoted in Andreas Lorenz, "The Influence of Taoism in Communist China," *Spiegel* Online, February 9, 2007, www.spiegel.de.

Chinese New Year

The most important and anticipated festival in China is Chinese New Year, also called the Spring Festival. The celebration begins on the first day of the first lunar month, which usually falls in January or February. Festivities continue for more than two weeks. No matter the distance, people from all corners of China rush to get home and reunite with family and friends. Freezing conditions cannot deter holiday travelers in airports and railway stations. Traditionally, Chinese New Year celebrates the end of winter, the beginning of the spring growing season, and the awakening of the earth.

Two weeks before the festival, children's eyes light up at the sight of shops, restaurants, and office buildings decked out in red and gold garlands and globe-like red lanterns. At this time of year, mandarin trees and plum blossoms spring up everywhere, and are considered a sign of good luck. Even the most well-behaved kids begin to fidget at the thought of all the festivities to come. Greetings of "*kung hei fat choi*" ("I wish you prosperity") are heard everywhere. Each Chinese New Year is also marked out with its own animal sign from the zodiac, and depictions of this animal become part of the decorating scheme. For example, 2017 was the Year of the Fire Rooster. Toddlers received bright red rooster dolls, and shop windows were festooned with large rooster paintings. Homes are decorated with red and gold banners bearing New Year messages of good fortune.

On New Year's Eve families get together for a huge reunion dinner, complete with favorite stir-fried dishes of rice, chicken, pork, fresh vegetables, and spicy seasonings. According to one superstition, all knives must be put away so that good luck is not cut off for the year. At midnight the fireworks begin, spectacular displays that are fitting for the nation that invented the firecracker. Children ring bells and twirl sparklers. The following day family members give the house a thorough cleaning to sweep out ill fortune for the year ahead. On New Year's Day parents and relatives give kids gifts of lucky money in bright red envelopes. Tech-savvy teens set up red envelope apps so family gifts of cash can be transferred digitally. Chinese youths also are taught to pay debts and resolve disputes with friends in order to start the New Year with a clean slate.

For the next few days, there will be more fireworks and servings of traditional foods such as rice cakes, sweet rice balls, spring rolls, and dumplings. In cities like Shanghai and Beijing, Buddhist temples are filled with young and old Chinese. They pay respects to their ancestors and solicit good fortune in the months to come. Downtown streets host ceremonial dances like the Dragon Dance and Lion Dance. A dozen or more performers carry poles inside the dragon, which is made of silk, paper, and bamboo. They raise and lower their sections in turn, making the dragon swerve and lurch as it winds its way through the streets, scaring away evil spirits. The lion contains two dancers who animate the elaborate head and body with acrobatic moves taken from martial arts. Gongs, drums, and horns accompany these colorful street processions.

In recent years Chinese students have grown more blasé about the Spring Festival, as they prefer to call it. They choose to sleep late, surf the Internet, and gather with friends instead of joining their families for the celebration. As the website History.com notes, "For some members of the younger generation the holiday has evolved from an opportunity to renew family ties to a chance for relaxation from work."[49]

The Lantern Festival and the Hungry Ghost Festival

Marking the end of Chinese New Year, the Lantern Festival is celebrated on city streets and in parks with music and dancing. Traditionally, it begins on the first full moon of the new year. Crowds parade down the street holding their lanterns aloft. Some lanterns

Actors perform the Dragon Dance during a parade to celebrate the Lantern Festival in the city of Chongqing. Marking the end of the Chinese New Year, the Lantern Festival is celebrated on city streets and parks across China.

are works of art, painted with flowers, birds, zodiac signs, and legendary scenes. Children carry brightly colored paper lanterns of every shape, from globes to cartoon animals. As night falls, battery-operated lights give the lanterns a vibrant glow. In the midst of the celebration, both children and adults play the Lantern Riddle Game. A lantern owner writes a riddle on a small sheet of paper and posts it inside the lantern. The riddles can be challenging, dealing with an historical topic or some clever use of Chinese characters. If a player can guess the correct answer, he or she wins a small prize, such as a toy or a bag of candy. Meanwhile, performers in the street do the Dragon Dance or walk on stilts as fireworks burst overhead.

A popular family tradition of the Lantern Festival is eating glutinous rice balls called *tangyuan*. The balls, representing family unity, are filled with sweet red bean paste or peanut butter. For many Chinese people, the taste and texture of these rice balls bring back vivid memories of childhood and family reunions.

Ancestor worship is the focus of the Hungry Ghost Festival, which falls in July or August on the traditional calendar. The ancient Chinese believed the seventh month is when restless ghosts come back to the earth to haunt the living. To avoid the ghosts' anger, at dusk a family will place their ancestors' images, paintings, and photos on a table near some burning incense. Plates of food are offered to the hungry ghosts, and a seat is left open at the table.

Religion Among Young Chinese

Festivals and holidays in China are mostly based on traditional beliefs related to Taoism and Buddhism that reach back for centuries. Most young Chinese people enjoy the customs and rituals without embracing the religious aspect. But surprising numbers of youths today are turning to religion, especially Christianity and Islam. Among Chinese under age thirty, 22.4 percent are Muslims and 22 percent Catholics, according to a 2015 survey conducted by Renmin University. The number of Muslims, in particular, seems certain to rise. "Islam tends to have a younger demographic," says Wei Dedong, a professor of Buddhist studies at Renmin. "Most believers of Islam belong to ethnic minority groups and it is

Megachurch in Atheist China

The brightly lit steeple and huge cross of Chongyi Church in Hangzhou, China, can be seen for miles around. Like megachurches in the United States, it caters to hip young churchgoers with a busy schedule. It is open seven days a week, and its clergy members are always ready to listen to parishioners. The sanctuary, which seats five thousand, features large video screens and speakers that rattle the walls with upbeat rock music. Coffee bars with snacks provide a casual atmosphere. Open seats can be hard to find on Sundays. All this exists in a nation that closely regulates churches and mosques, a nation that is officially atheist.

Chongyi is one of China's legal churches, operating according to government regulations and subject to certain government controls. The state stopped making an official count of Chinese Protestants in 1999, but observers believe the number has risen to more than 80 million. Should growth continue at the present pace, there could be 245 million by 2030, making China the most populous Christian nation in the world. Whether the Communist Party will continue to be as accepting of churches like Chongyi is an open question. In some cities the government has stepped in with cranes to remove giant crosses from the landscape. "They can take the cross from our church," says one junior pastor, "but they can't take it from our hearts."

Quoted in Robert Marquand, "In China, a Church-State Showdown of Biblical Proportions," *Christian Science Monitor*, January 11, 2015. www.csmonitor.com.

common for a woman to give birth to several children."[50] Dedong believes these children will almost certainly grow up to practice Islam themselves.

These statistics are potentially a problem for the Communist Party. Although the Chinese constitution protects religious freedom, the government promotes atheism as China's official philosophy, and religious groups are heavily regulated. No outside faith is allowed to challenge Communist rule. One ordinance prohibits government workers from practicing any religion.

Experts note that today's young people know little about the harsh campaigns against religion during Mao's Cultural Revolution. They grew up in a fast-paced consumer society that places great value on material wealth. But now, despite all their hard work and struggle for success, somehow they feel empty

Young worshippers take part in a Christmas Eve Catholic mass in Chengdu in southwest China. Most young people in China enjoy religious customs and rituals without embracing the religion, but increasing numbers are turning to Christianity and Islam.

inside. Liang Xingyang, a Taoist priest from Shaanxi Province, says young people are reaching out for something more fulfilling. "People have fewer material worries," he says. "It's not surprising that young people are turning their attention to their spiritual well-being."[51]

Unregistered Churches

As a result of this spiritual quest, the number of churches throughout China has grown rapidly. Many of them remain proudly unregistered and filled with young worshippers. The number of Protestants in China today is estimated at 60 million, and two-thirds of them belong to so-called underground churches. A typical example is the Early Rain Reformed Church in the southwestern city of Chengdu, led by a charismatic young pastor named Wang Yi. The church operates in a shabby office park. A police officer comes by every few days to get the names and personal information of any new people who show up, part of the government's policy of keeping tabs on religious believers, who are seen as potential troublemakers. Before the service, cheerful young men and women file in from work or school, some clutching Bibles, and take their seats in simple folding chairs. In his sermon—a eulogy for one of his favorite parishioners, an old woman called Auntie Wei—Wang Yi makes sure to stress the Lord's superiority over the Communist Party. As reporter Ian Johnson describes it:

> "People have fewer material worries. It's not surprising that young people are turning their attention to their spiritual well-being."[51]
>
> —Liang Xingyang, a Taoist priest from Shaanxi Province

Suddenly people were smiling; this was why they came to Early Rain Reformed Church. It was different from the anodyne [inoffensive] churches sponsored by the state. It was warm and direct, but most of all it was relevant. It was for people who didn't want the status quo, who were searching for alternatives to the life around them. Wang Yi was dressed in a suit, with short cropped hair and an earnest expression—a nice, modern young man, a perfect son-in-law. And yet here he was standing in front of them, telling them directly how to challenge the official way of looking at their country.[52]

A Wide Range of Beliefs

Today's young Chinese seem determined to turn away from settled customs and beliefs and find their own way in the world.

As one anonymous student writes in an online forum, "Chinese (nationality) people account for about 20% of the world's population. There are also more than 50 million Chinese (ethnicity) people in various countries. Regardless of which god you're referring to, there's probably a Chinese person that believes in it."[53] Time will tell how the government will react to the upsurge in various forms of religious belief among young people in China. The Communist Party has been successful up till now in loosening the reins just enough to maintain order. But a generation so used to working hard for a distant goal is unlikely to stop striving for new freedoms.

SOURCE NOTES

Chapter One: A Rising Nation

1. Quoted in Eric Fish, "China's Youth Admire America Far More than We Knew," *Foreign Policy*, February 9, 2017. http://for eignpolicy.com.

2. Quoted in AsiaNews.it, "Consultative Conference: 'The Government Must End the One-Child Rule,'" March 16, 2007. www.asianews.it.

3. Quoted in Chris Weller, "Here's China's Genius Plan to Move 250 Million People from Farms to Cities," Business Insider, August 5, 2015. www.businessinsider.com.

4. Quoted in Mick Brown, "Chongqing, the World's Fastest Growing City," *Telegraph* (London), July 12, 2009. www.tele graph.co.uk.

5. Quoted in Leslie T. Chang, *Factory Girls: From Village to City in a Changing China*. New York: Spiegel & Grau, 2008.

6. Richard Rigby, "From Tiananmen to Today," East Asia Forum, June 4, 2014. www.eastasiaforum.org.

7. Lily Han, "How Do Chinese People Feel About the Government of the People's Republic of China?," Quora, September 21, 2014. www.quora.com.

8. Howard W. French, "Middle Kingdom Millennials," *Wall Street Journal*, April 21, 2017. www.wsj.com.

Chapter Two: Family Life

9. Quoted in *South China Morning Post* (Hong Kong), "The Battle of China's Invisible Children, Victims of the One-Child Policy, to Recover Lost Years," December 26, 2016. www .scmp.com.

10. François de Martrin-Donos, "Why Is Family So Important in China?," *Medium* (blog), February 4, 2014. https://medium .com.

11. Quoted in Linda Poon, "Some Chinese Grandparents Are Making Their Grandkids Fat," NPR, July 29, 2015. www.npr .org.

12. Anonymous, "Is Ancestor Worship Still Popular with Chinese People?," Quora, February 25, 2017. www.quora.com.

13. Jennifer Hu, "Traditions: Why Do Asians Take Their Shoes Off When Entering a House?," Quora, October 11, 2015. www .quora.com.

14. "Chinese Greeting: 'Have You Eaten Already?,'" Travel China Guide, October 18, 2007. https://community.travelchina guide.com.

15. Quoted in *China-Memo.com* (blog), "Real Chinese Food Breakfast," November 12, 2017. www.china-memo.com.

16. theslimreaper2, "Are Your Folks Still Guilt-Tripping You with the 'I Created/Feed/House You' Excuse to Get You to Do Things?," Reddit, May 11, 2017. www.reddit.com.

17. Quoted in Carmen Fishwick, "China's 'Loneliest Generation': What It Was like Growing Up Under the One-Child Policy," *Guardian* (Manchester), December 7, 2015. www.theguard ian.com.

18. Quoted in Fishwick, "China's 'Loneliest Generation.'"

19. Linka, "How Does It Feel to Live in Rural China?," Quora, March 30, 2015. www.quora.com.

Chapter Three: School Life and Jobs

20. Quoted in Jeffrey Hays, "School Life in China," Facts and Details, 2013. http://factsanddetails.com.

21. Quoted in Hays, "School Life in China."

22. Quoted in Charlene Tan, *Learning from Shanghai: Lessons on Achieving Educational Success*. New York: Springer Science & Business Media, 2013, p. 113.

23. Quoted in Tan, *Learning from Shanghai*, p. 114.

24. Philip Kennicott, "Of Tykes and Tyrants: Elementary Democracy," *Washington Post*, June 13, 2007. www.washington post.com.

25. Echo Lu, "3 Big Differences Between Chinese and American Classroom Culture," *We Are IU* (blog). https://weareiu.com.

26. Quoted in *Dalian Diary* (blog), "12 Differences Between Chinese Education and American Education," June 1, 2007. https://slkchina.wordpress.com.

27. Peter Hessler, "The Wonder Years," *New Yorker*, March 31, 2008. www.newyorker.com.

28. Quoted in Sarah Butrymowicz, "A Day in the Life of Chinese Students," *HechingerEd* (blog), May 12, 2011. http://hechingered.org.

29. Alec Ash, "Is China's Gaokao the World's Toughest School Exam?," *Guardian* (Manchester), October 12, 2016. www.theguardian.com.

30. Quoted in Edward Wong, "Test That Can Determine the Course of Life in China Gets a Closer Examination," *New York Times*, June 30, 2012. www.nytimes.com.

31. Katherine Liu, "I Suffer from Post-Gaokao Stress Disorder," *Global Times* (Beijing), February 6, 2014. www.globaltimes.cn.

32. Ruoyu Liu, "How Is College Life like for a University Student in China?," Quora, March 18, 2017. www.quora.com.

33. Quoted in Xiaoqing Pi, "Dreams Collide with China Slowdown for Job-Seeking Graduates," Bloomberg, July 2, 2015. www.bloomberg.com.

34. Quoted in Xiaoqing Pi, "Dreams Collide with China Slowdown for Job-Seeking Graduates."

35. Quoted in *China Daily* (Beijing), "Chinese Graduates Face Tough Job-Hunting Season," July 9, 2015. www.chinadaily.com.cn.

Chapter Four: Social Life and Marriage

36. Quoted in Michelle Florcruz, "China's 'Diaosi': Growing 'Loser' Population Sheds Light on Chinese Youth," *International Business Times*, December 4, 2014. www.ibtimes.com.

37. Lu-Hai Liang, "It's Not Communism Holding China's Youth Back. It's Their Parents," *Foreign Policy*, April 3, 2017. http://foreignpolicy.com.

38. Joseph Wang, "Why Has China's Government Banned Facebook, Twitter, YouTube, Etc?," June 29, 2014, Quora. www.quora.com.

39. Clément Renaud, "What Is the Typical Teenage Life like in China Today?," Quora, August 15, 2015. www.quora.com.

40. Quoted in Peter Foster, "Western Companies Use Rock Music to Tap into China's Youth Market," *Telegraph* (London), November 20, 2009. www.telegraph.co.uk.

41. Quoted in Jeffrey Hays, "Chinese Youth: Teenagers and Young Adults in China," Facts and Details, 2013. http://factsanddetails.com.

42. Quoted in Jeffrey Hays, "Dating in China: Dating Services, TV and the Internet," Facts and Details, 2013. http://factsanddetails.com.

43. Quoted in Brook Larmer, "In a Changing China, New Matchmaking Markets," *New York Times*, March 9, 2013. www.nytimes.com.

44. Quoted in Clarissa Sebag-Montefiore, "Meet the 'Lover-Hunters' Who Help Male Chinese Millionaires Find a Wife," *Telegraph* (London), October 22, 2013. www.telegraph.co.uk.

45. Quoted in Roseann Lake, "It's Hard to Say 'I Love You' in Chinese," ChinaFile, February 14, 2014. www.chinafile.com.

Chapter Five: Holidays and Religious Life

46. Quoted in Quora, "What Is Double 11 in China? Is It a Famous Festival?," November 16, 2016. www.quora.com.

47. Quoted in Quora, "What Is Double 11 in China?"

48. Quoted in Quora, "Why Would Many Chinese People Like to Celebrate Western Festivals like Santa but Are Not Interested in Traditional Festivals?," January 8, 2015. www.quora.com.

49. History.com, "Chinese New Year," 2017. www.history.com.

50. Quoted in Monica Cantilero, "Islam, Catholicism seeing Rapid Growth Among Young People in China—Survey," Christian Today, July 13, 2015. www.christiantoday.com.

51. Quoted in Esther Teo, "More Young Chinese Embracing Religion," *Straits Times* (Singapore), August 1, 2015. www.straitstimes.com.

52. Ian Johnson, "In China, Unregistered Churches Are Driving a Religious Revolution," *Atlantic*, April 23, 2017. www.theatlantic.com.

53. Quoted in Quora, "Do Chinese People Believe in God?," May 10, 2015. www.quora.com.

Books

Alec Ash, *Wish Lanterns: Young Lives in New China*. London: Picador, 2017.

Mei Fong, *One Child: The Story of China's Most Radical Experiment*. New York: Houghton Mifflin Harcourt, 2016.

Ian Johnson, *The Souls of China: The Return of Religion After Mao*. New York: Pantheon, 2017.

Evan Osnos, *Age of Ambition: Chasing Fortune, Truth, and Faith in the New China*. New York: Farrar, Straus & Giroux, 2015.

Yong Zhao, *Who's Afraid of the Big Bad Dragon? Why China Has the Best (and Worst) Education System in the World*. San Francisco: Wiley, 2014.

Internet Sources

Alec Ash, "Is China's Gaokao the World's Toughest School Exam?," *Guardian* (Manchester), October 12, 2016. www.the guardian.com/world/2016/oct/12/gaokao-china-toughest-school -exam-in-world.

Antonia Blumberg, "Inside China's Secret Churches: How Christians Practice Their Faith Under an Atheist Government," *Huffington Post*, October 17, 2014. www.huffingtonpost.com /2014/10/16/china-secret-churches_n_5997532.html.

Meera Senthilingam, "How Quickly Can China Come Back from Its One-Child Policy?," CNN, October 13, 2016. www.cnn.com /2016/10/13/health/china-one-child-policy-population-growth.

Kristie Lu Stout, "China's Millennials: Under Pressure and Pushing Back," CNN, May 25, 2016. www.cnn.com/2016/05/25/asia /on-china-millennials-klustout.

Engen Tham and Adam Jourdan, "Meet the Ma Family: How Millennials Are Changing the Way China Thinks About Money," Reuters, December 12, 2016. www.reuters.com/article/us-china -debt-millennials-idUSKBN14015H.

Websites

Countries and Their Cultures: China (www.everyculture.com /Bo-Co/China.html). This website offers an extensive overview of China and its culture, including sections on demography, history, food and economy, education, family life, and political life.

Country Reports: China (www.countryreports.org/country/Chi na.htm). This informational website covers almost every aspect of Chinese customs and culture, including language, fashion, family life, student life, and socializing.

Facts and Details: Chinese Youth: Teenagers and Young Adults in China (http://factsanddetails.com/china/cat4/sub21 /item1878.html). Facts and Details presents a wealth of information related to Chinese youth and their lives in modern China. Among the topics addressed are Chinese youth culture, problems with obese teens, selfishness among only children, and political views among young Chinese.

World Education News & Reviews: Education in China (http:// wenr.wes.org/2016/03/education-in-china-2). This site examines China's educational system in detail, with informative graphics and a detailed look at each level of Chinese education.

INDEX

PICTURE CREDITS

ABOUT THE AUTHOR

John Allen is a writer who lives and works in Oklahoma City.